This **igloo book** belongs to:

....

igloobooks

Published in 2020
First published in the UK by Igloo Books Ltd
An imprint of Igloo Books Ltd
Cottage Farm, NN6 0BJ, UK
Owned by Bonnier Books
Sveavägen 56, Stockholm, Sweden
www.igloobooks.com

1120 004
8 10 12 13 11 9
ISBN 978-1-78197-631-9

Illustrated by Mike Byrne

Printed and manufactured in China

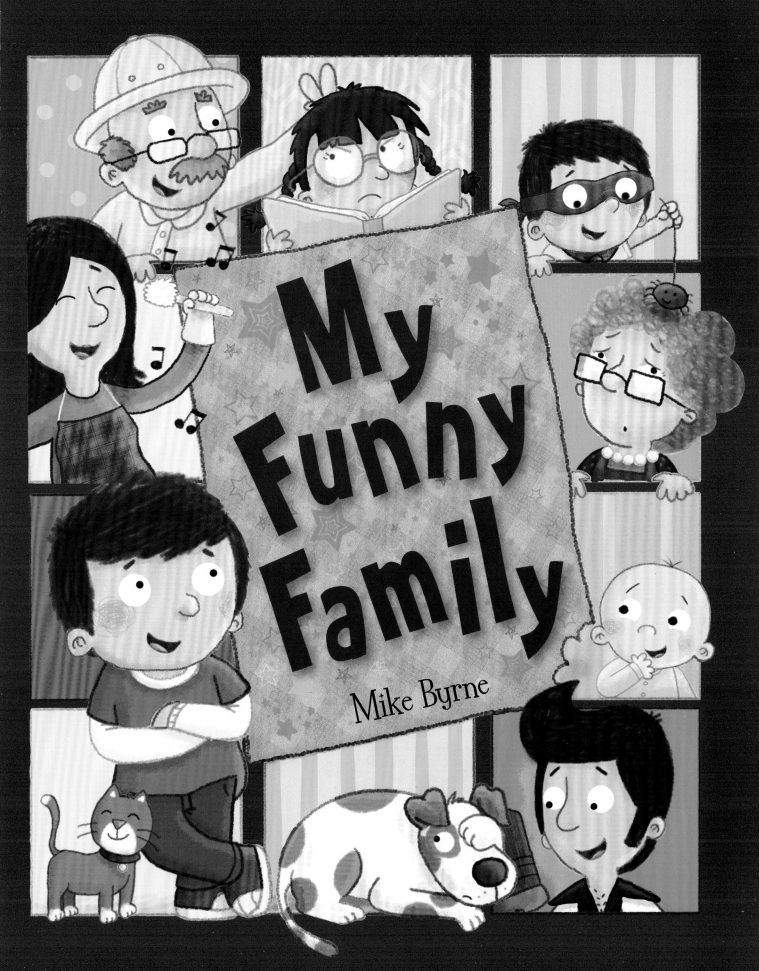

My Funny Family

Mike Byrne

igloobooks

In my funny family, there's my mum, my dad and me,
my sister, brother, Granny, Grandad and little Baby Lee.

There are two more in my family
who I must not forget,

Fido the dog and Kitty the cat,
my very special pets.

Mum's always busy washing up, there's loads of it to do.
She sings away, it's really loud, then Baby Lee sings, too!

Lee's singing turns to screaming,
you could hear him on the moon!
It's loud enough to shatter glass.
Mum, please stop singing soon.

My **dad** thinks he's a pop star
and he sings into a broom.
He bounces on the sofa
and he jumps around the room.

My brother, Tom, thinks Dad is cool
and dances on the floor.
Then, he shouts, "It's hero time!"
and he dashes out the door.

Tom's a superhero and he wears a cool, red mask.
Fido is his trusty friend. He's perfect for the task.

"Someone's in trouble!" my brother shouts,
"Super-Tom away!"
Then, Super-Tom and Wonder-Dog
are off to save the day.

My sister, Lily, is so smart.
In class she's always top.
She does big sums and reads a lot.
Dad says she'll never stop.

Fido thinks Lily's boring,
reading books and stuff all day,
but she helps me with my homework,
so I guess that she's okay.

Grandad's an explorer,
he's got a fancy hat.
He dresses **Fido** like a lion
and tries to trap the cat.

Grandad waves his hunter's net. It swishes around his head.
Forget about **Fido**, **Grandad**. Look, there's something in the shed!

When **Granny** bakes a birthday cake, she gets stuff everywhere.
She drops the eggs and milk and then gets icing in her hair.

Sometimes, Granny lets me help, which I quite like to do.
Then afterwards, our hungry pets can lick up all the goo!

When **Baby Lee** is quiet,
he's really good as gold,
but when he's being naughty,
he won't do what he is told.

Lee rides around on Fido,
while he throws his toys about.
"It's nearly bedtime," says my mum.
"He'll soon be tired out."

Fido loves to dig big holes,
the lawn looks very bumpy.
He's buried all my **sister's** things
and made her really grumpy.

My robot toy is filthy
and **Mum's** lost her mobile phone.
The only thing he hasn't buried
is his yummy bone.

We're on a family outing
and the picnic's under way.
Mum is singing, Dad is dancing,
Tom is saving the day!

The **baby** cries, the **kitten** sleeps, my **sister** reads a book.
Grandad sneaks up on a snail to take a closer look.

I love my **funny family** and I know that they love me,
and when we're all together, we're as happy as can be.